AF604696

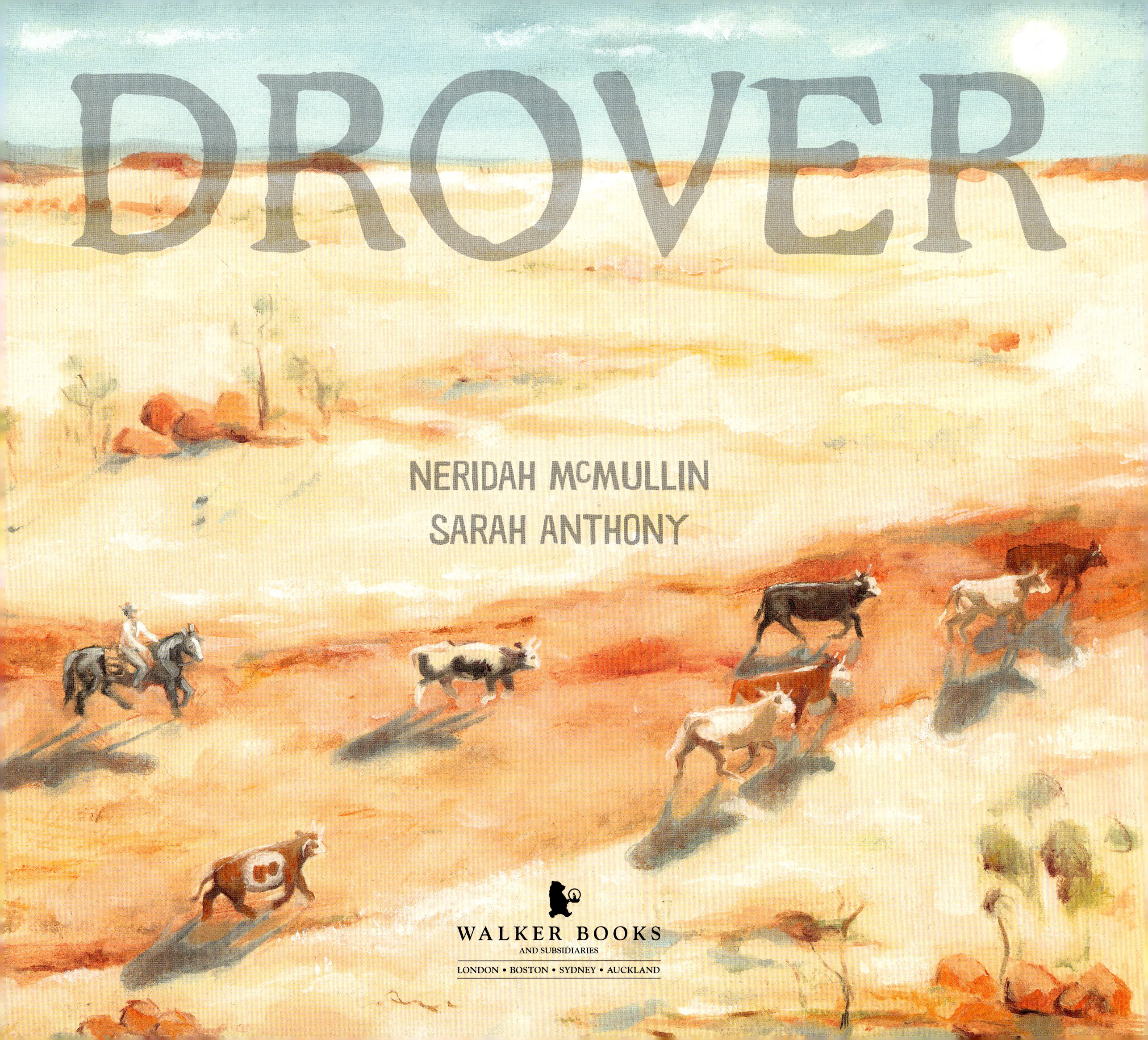

DROVER

NERIDAH McMULLIN

SARAH ANTHONY

WALKER BOOKS
AND SUBSIDIARIES
LONDON • BOSTON • SYDNEY • AUCKLAND

Drover reins in Midnight
and sighs at the peachy dawn.

The cattle have been quiet overnight,
but it's time to wake everyone and break camp.

The bullocks grumble,
but head off at a steady pace.

Drover rides in the lead.

Billy and Splinter are on the flanks
and Bib comes up the rear.
Cook and Andy go ahead
to set up the next camp.

By now, Drover has worked out the leaders and the troublemakers.

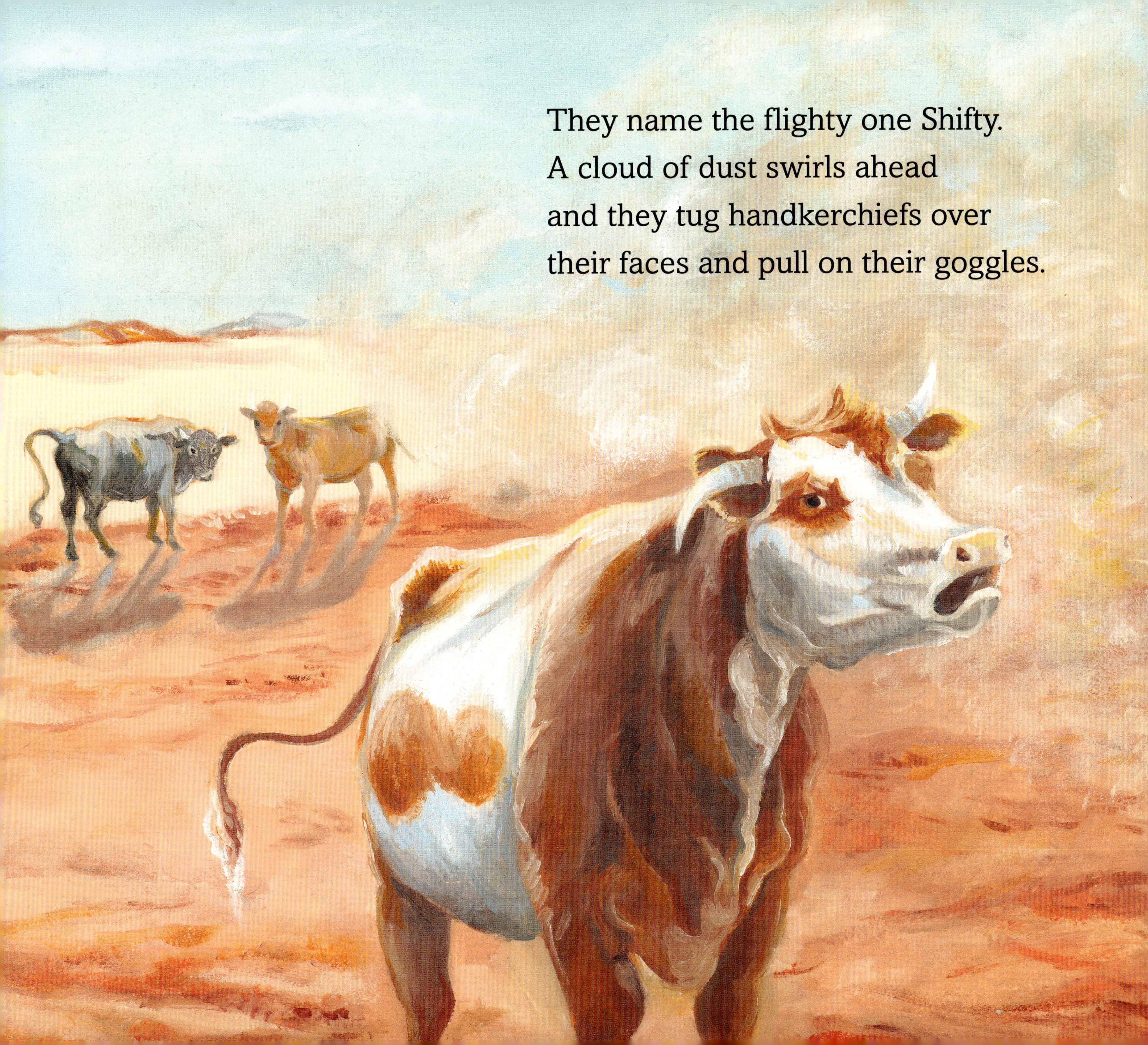

They name the flighty one Shifty.
A cloud of dust swirls ahead
and they tug handkerchiefs over
their faces and pull on their goggles.

It’s a dry day today and
the bullocks won’t get
water until tomorrow
morning when they
reach the next well.

Drover knows a full belly will help them forget their thirst and lets them graze as they walk.

As the sun rises high,
sweat prickles on their brows.
Flies cluster on their backs and
the bullocks toss their heads,
swatting at them with their tails.

Finding shade,
they rest during the
heat of the day. A hush
descends over the bush.

Lancewood is dense
with gnarly branches
with thorns so sharp
they can tear the clothes
off a rider and skewer
the horse.

Late in the afternoon they walk on,
arriving at camp before dusk.
Drover nods. The area is sheltered and clear.
If the bullocks are agitated and thirsty,
it doesn't take much to set off a rush –
a snapped twig could do it.

While the bullocks feed, they hobble the horses and the drovers dine like kings on corned beef, potatoes and onions, jam and damper. Around the campfire, they yarn.

Bib's on first watch and Drover settles down to sleep,
smiling as Bib sings softly out of tune.

The desert air chills and Bib brings the bullocks in close.
They lie down near the fire, letting out a huff
as they fall asleep.

Drover loves this sound and has never felt more content,
under a canopy of a million stars
in this wide-open, fenceless country.

At two in the morning, Drover feels a scurry across the blanket.

The drovers are on their feet before their eyes are even open. Shifty has bolted in fright, blindly tearing off into the inky night.

Drover and Bib vault onto their horses, taking off at a gallop.

They chase the cattle,
racing to catch up with them,
racing to catch Shifty.

"Come on, Bib. Sing!"
hollers Drover.
"We've got to stop them
stampeding into the bush.
We'll never get them out."

They catch the herd
and charge up to the front.
Amidst the thundering of hooves
and heaving flanks, choking dust
and spittle fly through the air.

Drover and Midnight are
hurtling headlong into darkness.

Suddenly, Drover and Midnight are neck and neck with Shifty. Galloping side by side, drover tugs on Midnight's rein, asking her to lean in on Shifty.

At full tilt, they nudge and bump into each other, dangerously teetering.

Stride for stride, they race on until, at last, Shifty finally gives in and turns in on the herd.

The rest follow and circle in on themselves, milling and moving in a wide arc until they eventually slow to a walk.

They're huffing and puffing and bellowing to each other.

"What caused that?" Drover asks Splinter. "Bandicoot," says Splinter. Drover and Bib shake their heads.

The next day they walk the bullocks to the last bore, letting them fill their bellies before the last leg. Drover, Billy and Splinter do a head count and they haven't lost one bullock.

Bib, Cook and Andy catch up on the Bagman's Gazette – messages left on the water tanks by other drovers.

As they wheel the bullocks
into the town of Dajarra,
they find the streets are lined
with cheering people.

Drover sits a little straighter
in the saddle and cracks her whip
high above her as she gallops by.

They have travelled thousands of kilometres and been in the saddle for almost half a year and they're all bone-weary.

DAJARRA HOTEL

Edna is dreaming about
a hot bath and a soft bed,
but she knows she'll do it all over again,
as her heart belongs in the bush.

EDNA JESSOP (nee Zigenbine) was Australia's first female boss drover. In 1950, she took a herd of 1600 head of cattle from Western Australia to Queensland. For six months, they travelled through harsh country over a distance of 2240 kilometres. Edna began droving as a child, but on this trip she was in her early twenties. Her father, a boss drover, fell ill and Edna took over.

Photo credit Douglas Lockwood (1918-80) / *Edna Zigenbine* 1950 / Collection: Library and Archives Northern Territory

GLOSSARY

A DROVER is a person who guides livestock on long walks from farms to markets. Trips could take many months and were slow-going, winding through some of the most isolated and barren areas of Australia. They were incredibly dangerous, and many cattle, sheep and even some drovers have died while droving.

At the time of this story, one in four drovers was an Indigenous Australian, and they were famed for their stockmen skills.

BULLOCKS: male beef cattle, but not bulls.

LEADERS AND TROUBLEMAKERS: important for the stockmen to identify so as to keep control of the herd. It wasn't unusual for drovers to nickname their cattle. Travelling together for so long, they got to know each other well.

SHIFTY: untrustworthy.

DRY DAY: means the cattle won't drink water that day.

SINGING TO THE HERD: reassures and keeps the cattle calm at night.

WATCH: they all take turns to guard the herd, usually two-hour watches. Boss drover always takes the last one before dawn.

NIGHT HORSE: all droving plants have a "Night horse". Calm and surefooted, they have excellent night vision. They're used check the herds at night and to stop a rush.

RUSH: is an Australian word for a stampede.

BANDICOOTS: The Golden Bandicoot is a small, nocturnal marsupial.

MILLING: means to turn cattle in on themselves so they run in a circle. It's a technique to stop a rush. It's dangerous work, especially if a horse treads in a hole and falls in front of galloping herd.

BAGMAN'S GAZETTE: "newspaper" of the outback. They were written messages left by drovers on the sides of the water tanks at each bore and included news, gossip, complaints, quotes, poetry and pictures.
"Bagman" refers to "Swagman".

To Edna, and all drovers past & present
Thank you to Ian & Toby, and my parents,
John & Lynette Bade

– NM

Dedicated with love and thanks to my sons
Flynn, Charlie and Sam, and my mother
Diana Anthony.

– SA

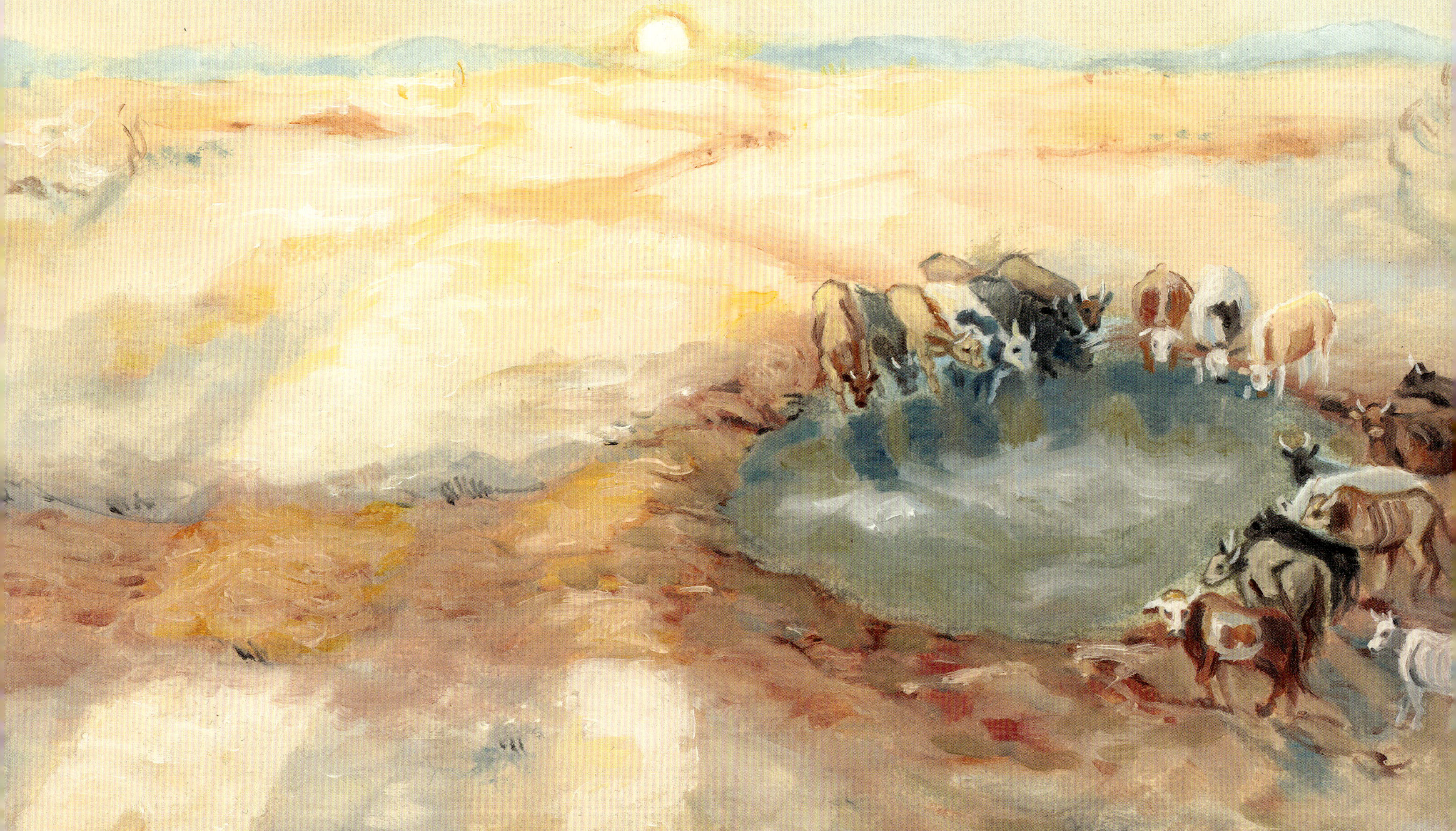

First published in 2021 by Walker Books Australia Pty Ltd
Locked Bag 22, Newtown
NSW 2042 Australia
www.walkerbooks.com.au

A catalogue record for this book is available from the National Library of Australia

ISBN: 978 1 760652 08 1

The illustrations for this book were created in oils
Typeset in Amasis Pro

Printed and bound in China

10 9 8 7 6 5 4 3 2 1